Expedition to the Internet

Linda Liukas

Feiwel and Friends
New York

For Pirjo, Heikki, Lotta, and Mikael, for all those years that I
kept the home modem occupied

A FEIWEL AND FRIENDS BOOK
An Imprint of Macmillan Publishing Group, LLC
175 Fifth Avenue, New York, NY 10010.

HELLO RUBY: EXPEDITION TO THE INTERNET. Copyright © 2018 by Linda Liukas.
All rights reserved. Printed in China by RR Donnelley Asia Printing Solutions Ltd.,
Dongguan City, Guangdong Province.

Our books may be purchased in bulk for promotional, educational, or business use. Please contact your local
bookseller or the Macmillan Corporate and Premium Sales Department at (800) 221-7945 ext. 5442 or by e-mail
at MacmillanSpecialMarkets@macmillan.com.

Library of Congress Cataloging-in-Publication Data is available.
ISBN 978-1-250-19599-9 (hardcover) / ISBN 978-1-250-19600-2 (ebook)

Feiwel and Friends logo designed by Filomena Tuosto
First Edition, 2018

3 5 7 9 10 8 6 4 2

mackids.com

Introduction for the Parent

This generation of kids grew up with computers and the Internet as part of its everyday life. Kids can chat online, create their own content, and play games over the Internet with friends on the other side of the world. Childhood increasingly happens online.

The Internet is something kids take for granted. But very few know what the Internet is and how it actually works. Is it a cloud or a bunch of cables? How does the information travel online? And why do you need people on the Internet?

In this story Ruby, Julia, and Django build a Snow Internet. On the Snow Internet, the kids do come across things that are a little frightening. But above all, they enjoy the expedition and sense of adventure.

This book is designed to be worked on together with a parent. You can start by reading the story. Then have a look at the six chapters in the activity book. Each chapter has a set of exercises that builds on the concepts of creativity. Spend time playing and replaying the exercises. It's normal and okay to make mistakes and look at the same problem in different ways. You can also go online and check out additional activities.

Toolboxes give information for parents and list concepts that are linked to the topic discussed. All concepts can be found in the glossary. You can find suggested answers from the answer key at helloruby.com.

My personal journey to the Internet started some twenty years ago. The Internet of my memories was more gentle and more anonymous. I had great adventures as Jedi Knight Sabe Sunrider and stayed busy building fansites for my idols.

The Internet has changed since my early experiences. Kids today need to learn how to navigate a more commercial Internet full of apps and ads. Then again, the future Internet might be something different—perhaps a copy machine, a runway, a time capsule, or a space shuttle.

"The world is changing,
a world no longer made
of islands, of intervals and spaces,
of oceans and mountains
but a world made like a web . . ."
—Loris Malaguzzi

Characters:

RUBY

I like learning new things and I hate giving up. I love to share my opinions.
Want to hear a few? My dad is the best. I tell great jokes. I'm a mischief-maker
and prefer my cupcakes without strawberries, please.

Secret superpower	I can imagine impossible things.	**Pet peeves**	I hate confusion.
Birthday	February 24	**Favorite expression**	Why?
Interests	Maps, secrets, codes, and small talk		

JULIA

I want to be a scientist when I grow up. I'm interested
in robotics. I have the smartest and cutest AI toy robot.
Ruby is my best friend, and Django is the best big
brother ever.

Secret superpower	I can do many things at the same time. Like a hundred!	**Pet peeves**	People jumping to conclusions
Birthday	February 14		
Interests	Science, math, India, bouncing	**Favorite expression**	Let me think it over.

DJANGO

I have a pet snake called Python. I'm very organized, persistent, and
somewhat rigid. I like things that can be counted: odd, even, prime,
cubed, rooted, backward, and forward. But I don't take myself too
seriously.

Secret superpower	I always have a solution.	**Pet peeves**	People crowding around me when I stand in line
Birthday	February 20		
Interests	The circus, philosophy, and pythonic things	**Favorite expression**	Simple is better than complex.

WEBSITES & APPS

300

404

BROWSERS

CLIENTS

200

ROUTER

DNS SERVERS

INTERNET
Class of
2018

SERVERS

CABLES

CELLULAR TOWER

Ruby and Julia are best friends. They go to the same school, live on the same street, and play together every day.

Sometimes Ruby and Julia get into fights.

"I can solve anything with my imagination," says Ruby.

"It is important to find the truth," explains Julia, who wants to be a scientist.

"Don't be a bore ball, Julia," Ruby snaps.

"You are being childish," Julia sighs, sounding like a grown-up.

But the quarrels never last long. Being best friends is so much more fun.

After school, Ruby and Julia are excited to go outside and play in the snow.

"What should we do?" Ruby asks while putting on her green winter boots.

"Let's build a castle out of snow," Julia suggests.

"That's a good idea! I know how to build a tower," Ruby says.

Outside, everything is covered with fresh snow.

"Should we make a snow angel?" Julia asks.

"No, I want to make a snow. . . ghost," Ruby giggles.

Julia is laughing, too.

"Ruby, you are such a Miss Snow-it-all."

"Snowball fight," shouts some-body behind the girls.

"That was mean," Ruby snaps, shaking the snow out of her hair.

"We don't want to play with you, Django. Julia and me are going to build a snow castle with a tower and other really cool things!"

"Like what?" Django asks.

"Like a . . . a . . . Snow Internet!" Ruby answers.

"A Snow Internet is a great idea," Julia says, giving her brother an angry look.

"It would be easier with more people," Django mutters.

"He's right," Julia admits. "Should we let him play?"

"Okay, but I'm in charge!" Ruby says.

Grabbing shovels, buckets, and string, they are ready to build the Snow Internet.

But where do they start?

"Should we build the Internet in the front garden?" Django asks.

"Internet is not a place," Ruby points out.

"Well, Ruby, you wanted to be in charge. What do you think the Internet is?" Django replies.

"The Internet is made up of all kinds of fun things," Ruby happily explains.

"Like cats and dancing hamsters and the greatest riddles. You can make a thousand new friends on the Internet and make a billion copies of yourself."

Julia also gets excited about the Internet.

"The Internet has towers and cables. It reaches as high as the satellites in the sky and dives as deep as the bottom of the ocean.

"On the Internet things move at the speed of light. And sometimes the Internet hides in a big cloud.

"The Internet is the world's greatest jungle gym," Julia concludes.

Finally, Django jumps in. "The Internet is great for surfing and sending information all around the world!"

"But how does the information know where to go?" Ruby asks.

"It follows the Internet traffic rules. Finding the destination is easy because everything on the Internet has its own address."

Ruby, Julia, and Django work hard for hours.

The Snow Internet is finally
taking shape, but . . .
   "It isn't quite what I expected,"
Ruby sighs.

"All the wires and cables are still missing," Julia says, trying to cheer Ruby up.
"And we need to put the addresses in place," Django adds.

Ruby thinks hard.
"I know!" she says.

27

"More friends! We need more friends for it to feel like the Internet! I'm going to go get the penguins."

Ruby is so excited she forgets that she isn't supposed to go to the river on her own. Especially not when it's already getting dark.

Ruby sees the penguins and
waves at them, but then something
beneath the ice catches her eye.

"Ruby! Are you okay?" Django asks. "We heard a loud noise and followed your tracks in the snow."

"It's all right now." Julia comforts Ruby, who has tears in her eyes.

Ruby nods and wipes away the tears. "The warning for the thin ice is there for a reason," Django says.

"We just have to be alert but not afraid," Julia says, giving Ruby a hug.

"Let's go back to the Snow Internet," Django suggests cheerfully.

"Is it ready now?" Ruby gasps.

SERVERS

"Oh, the Internet is wonderful!" Ruby exclaims.
"So many nice things!"

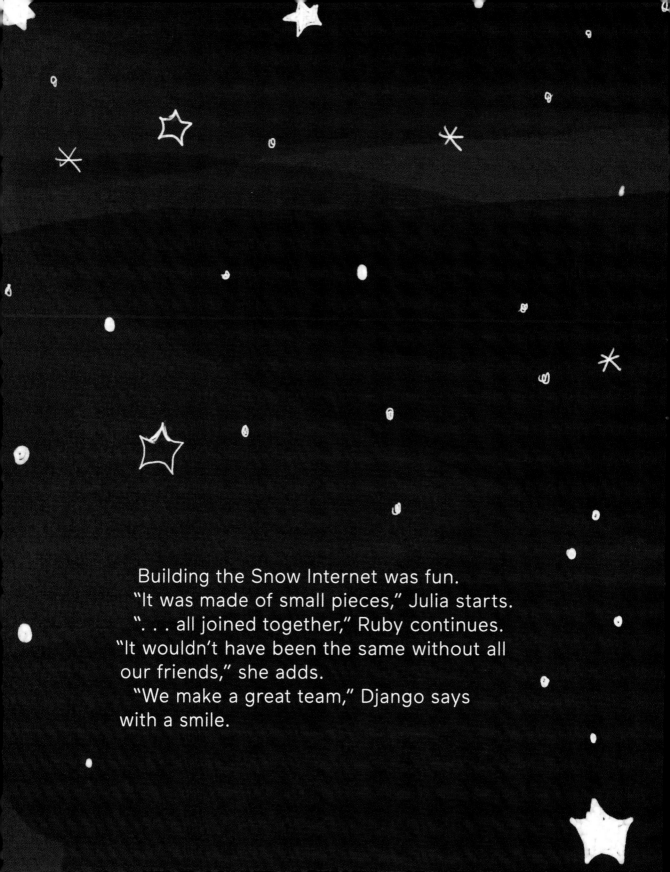

Building the Snow Internet was fun.
"It was made of small pieces," Julia starts.
". . . all joined together," Ruby continues.
"It wouldn't have been the same without all our friends," she adds.
"We make a great team," Django says with a smile.

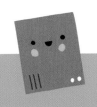

Activity Book

What is the Internet? Is it a place to chat with friends and play games like Ruby thinks? Or maybe a bunch of wires and cables, as Julia suggests? Or a way for different computers to talk to each other as Django thinks?

Pack your bags and get ready, because we'll be going on an expedition to the Internet.

1
WHAT IS THE INTERNET?

Ruby, Julia, and Django had fun building the Snow Internet, but the Internet is much more complicated.

The Internet is a huge network of computers all over the world. On the Internet the computers can talk to each other by moving data from one computer to another.

You can use the Internet to play games, chat, watch videos, send e-mail, browse websites, or shop online. Best of all, you can make new friends and learn new skills on the Internet.

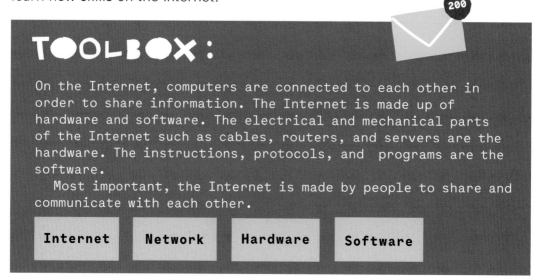

TOOLBOX:

On the Internet, computers are connected to each other in order to share information. The Internet is made up of hardware and software. The electrical and mechanical parts of the Internet such as cables, routers, and servers are the hardware. The instructions, protocols, and programs are the software.

Most important, the Internet is made by people to share and communicate with each other.

| Internet | Network | Hardware | Software |

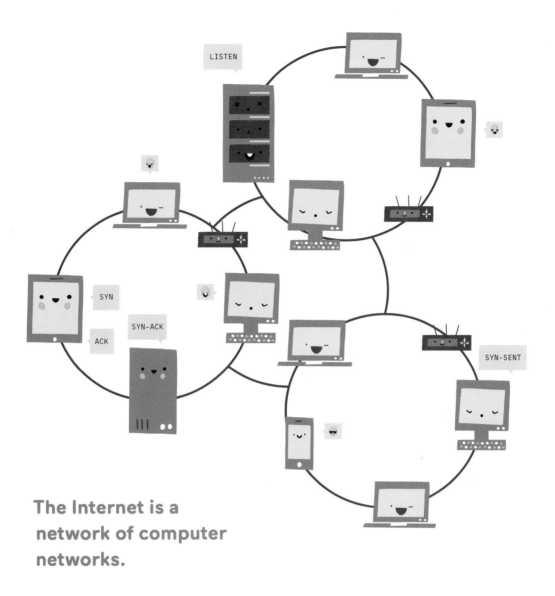

The Internet is a network of computer networks.

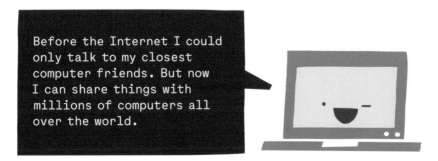

Before the Internet I could only talk to my closest computer friends. But now I can share things with millions of computers all over the world.

What Can You Do on the Internet?

You can use computers, laptops, phones, tablets, and game consoles to go online. But your alarm clock, washing machine, and favorite toy might also be connected to the Internet.

We use the Internet many times a day, often almost without noticing. Keep a log for one week of all the times you use the Internet. What are the things you do online? Then swap your log with a friend's and compare.

DAY	DEVICE	ACTIVITY

 Discuss

How could you do these things without using the Internet? Ask an adult what it was like to grow up without the Internet.

THIS IS HOW MANY TIMES I WENT ONLINE:

 Print out the log at **helloruby.com/play**

What Is the Internet Made Of?

Julia and Django are playing a game where each person collects things that are connected to the Internet. There are five items that aren't part of the Internet. Try to find them first! Don't step on those five circles.

- How many Internet items can you collect if you take the shortest route from Julia to Django?

- Try to find a route from Django to Julia that collects all the items that are part of the Internet.

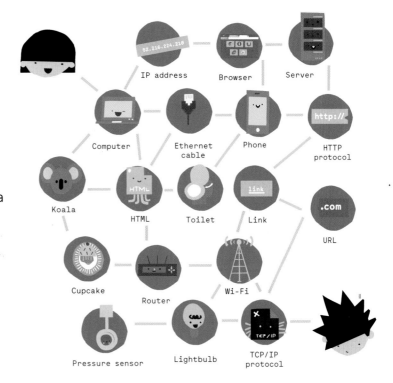

 **Discuss**

Which of the items are hardware and which ones are software?

What Are Networks?

Networks are everywhere around us. A network is really just a group of interconnected people or things.

Social networks

Family and school classes are examples of social networks, which are made up of people and the relationships between them. We can have social networks in real life and on the Internet.

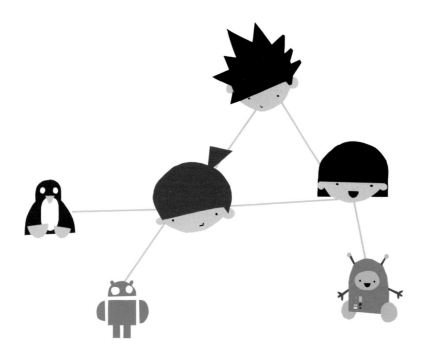

 # Discuss

What kinds of social networks are you a part of? Can you draw a picture of your family network? Why do people form networks?

Technical networks

There are also technical networks such as a railroad network, which consists of train stations that are connected to each other by trains and rails.

Look at the igloo village below. Each igloo should be connected to at least two others. Follow the line with your finger. Can you spot the missing connections?

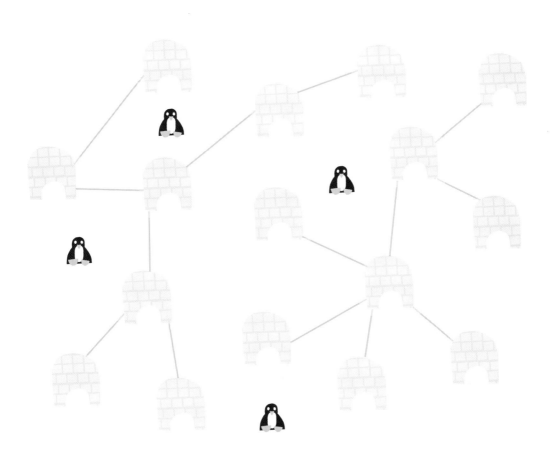

Computer Networks

There are many different ways computers can be connected. Here are some examples of different patterns for organizing computer networks.

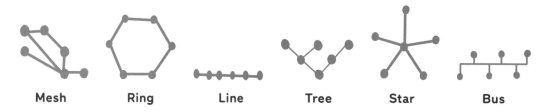

| Mesh | Ring | Line | Tree | Star | Bus |

Look at the computers on the next page. Can you find all the patterns shown above?

Hint: Take a piece of paper, put it on top of the page, then pick a color. Circle each computer of that color and then draw lines connecting the computers using one of the patterns above.

Name which network pattern belongs to which computer.

Now connect at least one computer from each network to a computer in another network. You've created a network of networks!

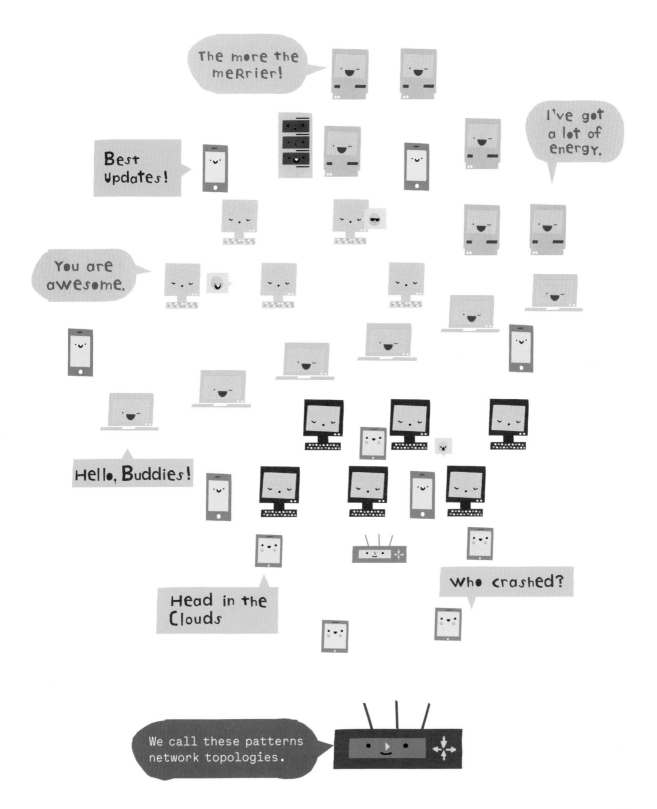

51

Add a Link

Links make it easy to navigate the Internet. By clicking or tapping a link you can jump to another document or Web page. Links can be words, pictures, or videos.

Ice-cream shop

Ruby wrote a post about her new ice-cream shop. She also made a video, a map, and a menu. Which words in Ruby's post might you link to each item?

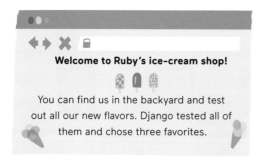

Welcome to Ruby's ice-cream shop!

You can find us in the backyard and test out all our new flavors. Django tested all of them and chose three favorites.

Video of Django

Map with address

Web page with a menu

Animal clinic

Julia wrote instructions on how to take care of a snow leopard who has a cold. Choose at least three words that you would make into links. Where would the different links lead? What kind of information would you find useful?

How to take care of a snow leopard with a cold

- Rub gently between the ears.
- Take its temperature.
- Check ears, paws, tail, and tummy.
- Give some cold milk and fruit.
- Make sure that the patient gets enough sleep.
- Read stories.
- Wait for three days before going out to play.

 Discuss

Find a newspaper article. Mark any words or pictures that could be useful links. Glue the article on a piece of paper and add a short description of the sites where the links could lead.

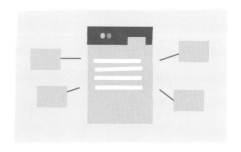

Draw the Internet

According to technical drawings, it's a cloud, an explosion, a star, or a weird lump. But no one really knows what the Internet looks like.

Draw a picture of your Internet. Can you place yourself in the picture? Where are you?

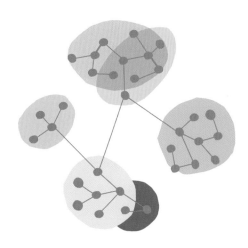

Draw something

H U G E

related to the Internet.

Draw something small related to the Internet.

Go to **helloruby.com/play** and see what other kids have drawn

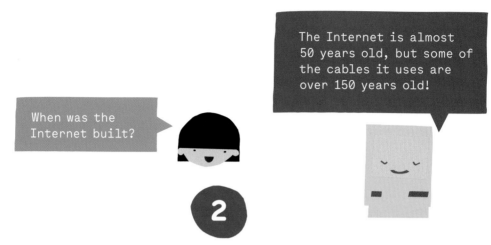

When was the Internet built?

The Internet is almost 50 years old, but some of the cables it uses are over 150 years old!

2

INFRASTRUCTURE OF THE INTERNET

Internet cables in the ground, undersea cables on the seabed, and wireless zones form a network that crosses oceans and reaches almost all countries in the world.

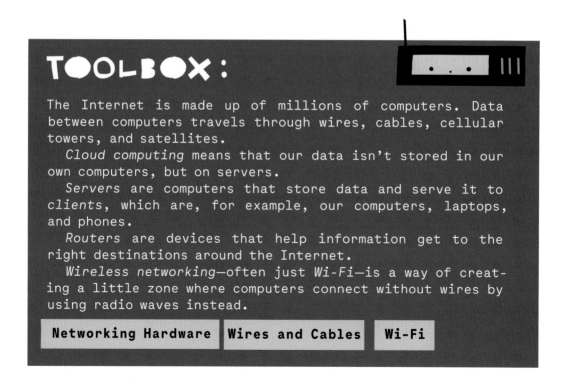

TOOLBOX:

The Internet is made up of millions of computers. Data between computers travels through wires, cables, cellular towers, and satellites.

Cloud computing means that our data isn't stored in our own computers, but on servers.

Servers are computers that store data and serve it to *clients*, which are, for example, our computers, laptops, and phones.

Routers are devices that help information get to the right destinations around the Internet.

Wireless networking—often just *Wi-Fi*—is a way of creating a little zone where computers connect without wires by using radio waves instead.

Networking Hardware   **Wires and Cables**   **Wi-Fi**

Hiding in Plain Sight

The Internet often feels invisible. But if you take a closer look, you will start noticing things that are a part of the Internet. Go on a walk around your home and neighborhood.

Connected devices

- All devices that use the Internet are a part of the Internet network. How many computers, laptops, and phones can you spot?
- What other things might be connected to the Internet in your home or neighborhood?
- Can you find your home router?

Cables

- Can you find any wires or cables that might have to do with the Internet?
- Draw a picture of your home or school with all the different wires and cables that belong to the Internet.

Look up and look down

- Look up to the trees or walls. Can you spot boxes that might have to do with the Internet?
- Look down at the street. Are there any manhole covers? Internet cables often hide underground.
- To go to the Internet you need an Internet connection. You can get it from an Internet service provider (ISP). Do you see any ads for ISPs?

Routers

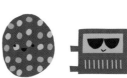

Manhole cover   Wi-Fi hot spot   ISP box

Exercise 8: Wires and Cables

Fixing Underwater Cables

Underwater cables are an important part of the Internet. There have been several reports of disruptions in Internet services, but repair ships and underwater submarine robots are ready to go out to fix things. Can you send each ship or submarine to the right destination? What is the corresponding letter and number of the coordinate on the map below?

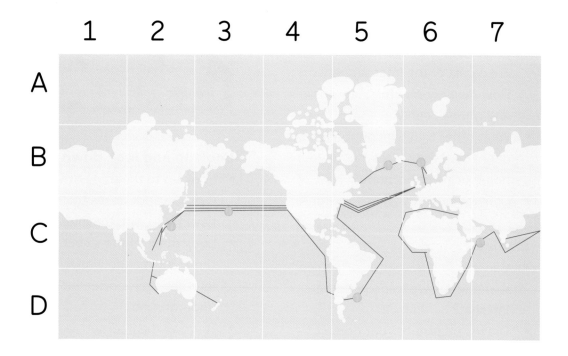

Discuss

Search for a map of the Internet and find out how the cables at the bottom of the oceans connect the different continents. Draw a picture of a repair ship at sea or an underwater robot fixing the cable on the seabed.

- Urgent repair work is needed in Japan.
- Send the pink underwater robot to:

- Sharks have bitten a cable connecting the US to Asia.
- Send the red ship to:

- An old cable needs to be replaced in Greenland. That's a job for a special underwater robot!
- Send the yellow underwater robot to:

- A long fishing line bearing hooks has damaged a cable near the Norwegian coast.
- Send the green ship to:

- An underwater volcano eruption off the easternmost corner of Africa is slowing down the Internet traffic in the region.
- Send the blue ship to:

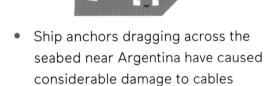

- Ship anchors dragging across the seabed near Argentina have caused considerable damage to cables there.
- Send the purple ship to:

Wi-Fi Hunt

In a Wi-Fi network, computers can connect to the Internet and to each other with radio waves, which are invisible. Every Wi-Fi network needs its own name. What would your network be called?

Draw what you imagine the Wi-Fi would look like as a character. Come up with a funny explanation about your character.

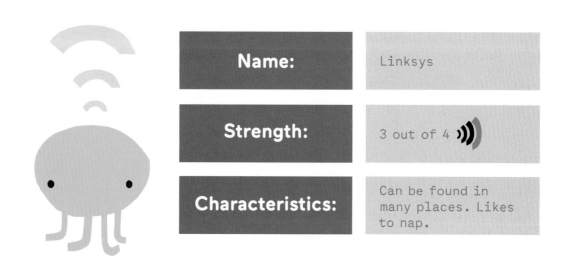

Name:	Linksys
Strength:	3 out of 4)))
Characteristics:	Can be found in many places. Likes to nap.

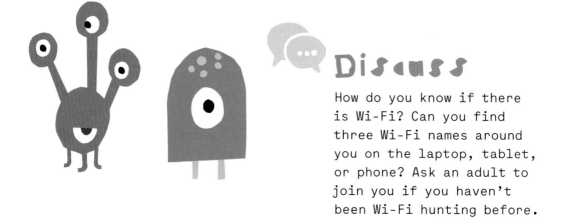

Discuss

How do you know if there is Wi-Fi? Can you find three Wi-Fi names around you on the laptop, tablet, or phone? Ask an adult to join you if you haven't been Wi-Fi hunting before.

Battle of Towers

Cell towers and smartphones link together!

- The aim of the game is to get three cell towers in a row, either horizontally, vertically, or diagonally.
- Each player needs three cell towers. Draw the cell tower pieces or use small coins.
- To start, take turns putting your three cell tower pieces on any of the outside dots. On each turn, a player moves one cell tower. Cell towers can be moved to any open dot on the board.
- The first player to get his or her three cell towers in a row wins.

Routing Work

Messages don't travel by only one route. They take many different paths through the millions of routers around the world. Most routers can move massive amounts of data in just milliseconds, but some are busier than others.

   The numbers between the routers tell how long it will take for the message to go through. Add up the numbers you pass. Which path from client computer to server will be the fastest? Which one will be the slowest?

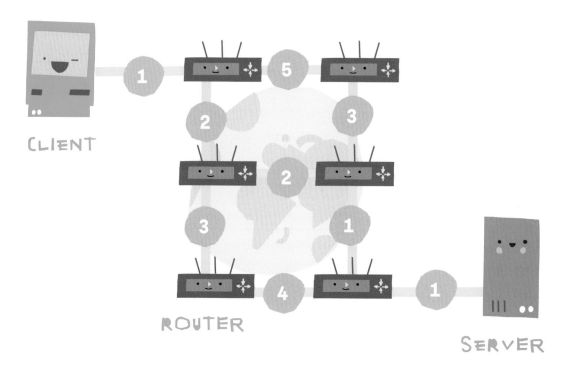

CLIENT

ROUTER

SERVER

Which path from client computer to server will be the fastest this time?

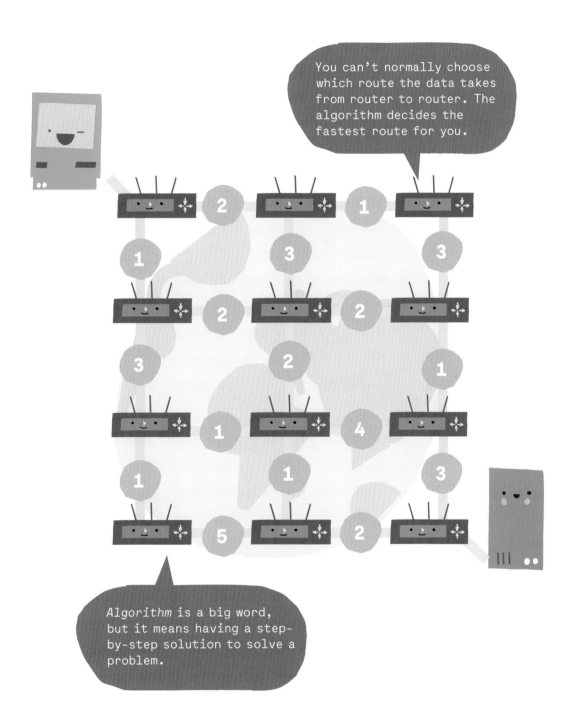

You can't normally choose which route the data takes from router to router. The algorithm decides the fastest route for you.

Algorithm is a big word, but it means having a step-by-step solution to solve a problem.

Exercise 12: Networking Hardware

Mixed-Up Servers

Servers contain things like e-mails, pictures, and websites. Servers are often connected to form big data centers in different parts of the world.

Oh no! The servers and clients have gotten mixed-up. Can you tell which server(s) each client visited?

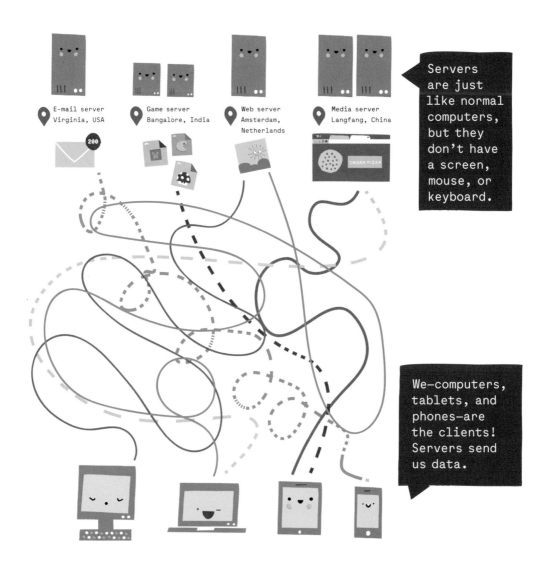

E-mail server
Virginia, USA

Game server
Bangalore, India

Web server
Amsterdam,
Netherlands

Media server
Langfang, China

Servers are just like normal computers, but they don't have a screen, mouse, or keyboard.

We—computers, tablets, and phones—are the clients! Servers send us data.

Speed of the Internet

To send messages, pictures, and videos through the Internet cables and networks, computers convert them to digital data. Digital data can move at the speed of light.

Tap each dot on your way around the world. Go as fast as you can! How many times can you go around the world in 10 seconds?

- **Me:** [   ] times around the world in 10 seconds

- **My friend:** [   ] times around the world in 10 seconds

- **Internet:** **50** times around the world in 10 seconds

Bandwidth means the amount of data that can be sent over your Internet connection per second.

Who decides how computers talk on the Internet?

The networking protocols are created by groups of people. It's a work in progress.

3

PROTOCOLS OF THE INTERNET

In the past, every computer spoke in its own way. But on the Internet computers use the same set of rules for talking to each other. This is called a protocol.

TOOLBOX:

When computers send data to each other it is broken down into tens of thousands of small packets and sent across the Internet.

TCP/IP protocol is a set of rules each computer uses to talk to each other and send data back and forth. Every device on the Internet—also your computer and phone—has a unique IP address, which is made up of numbers. Computers use numric IP addresses, but for people it is easier to remember addresses that consist of words. These addresses are called URL addresses. DNS servers keep lists of all addresses and they can convert URL addresses to IP addresses.

Digital Data	Packet Switching and TCP/IP
IP Address	URL

What Does Information Look Like?

Computers can only process information that is in digital form. This means that all data is first turned into 1s and 0s. Instead of sending messages, pictures, or videos over the Internet, computers send data consisting of the numbers 1 and 0. A lot can be done with only two digits!

Take a piece of paper and put it on top of the picture. Color in the squares according to the rules.

What did you find? Can you make your own pixel character?

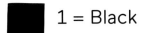 1 = Black

0 = Blue

00 = Yellow

			1	1	1	1	1	1	
		1	1	1	1	1	1	1	
	1	1	1	1	1	1	1	1	1
	1	1	1	1	1	1	1	1	1
	1	1	0	1	1	1	0	1	1
	1	1	1	1	00	1	1	1	1
	1	1	1	1	1	1	1	1	1
	1	1	1	0	0	0	1	1	1
	1	1	0	0	0	0	0	1	1
	1	0	0	0	0	0	0	1	1
	1	0	0	0	0	0	0	1	1
	1	0	0	0	0	0	0	1	1
00	00	0	0	0	00	00	00	1	1

Secret Messages

When you send your friend a message or picture over the Internet, the digital information is broken down into smaller chunks called packets. Packets are sent to the recipient through many different routes and then reassembled. Each packet includes information on the sender and the recipient and instructions on how the message fits together.

Can you help reassemble the messages from Ruby, Julia, and Django? Pay attention to the sequence so that you get the words in the message in the right order.

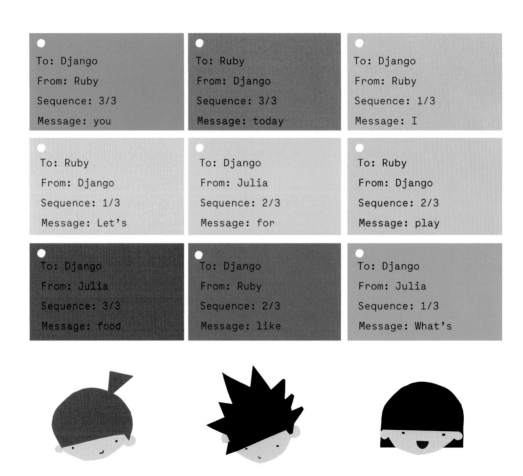

To: Django
From: Ruby
Sequence: 3/3
Message: you

To: Ruby
From: Django
Sequence: 3/3
Message: today

To: Django
From: Ruby
Sequence: 1/3
Message: I

To: Ruby
From: Django
Sequence: 1/3
Message: Let's

To: Django
From: Julia
Sequence: 2/3
Message: for

To: Ruby
From: Django
Sequence: 2/3
Message: play

To: Django
From: Julia
Sequence: 3/3
Message: food

To: Django
From: Ruby
Sequence: 2/3
Message: like

To: Django
From: Julia
Sequence: 1/3
Message: What's

Internet's Address Book

Computers use numeric IP addresses and people use URL addresses that are made up of words. DNS servers all over the world keep lists of IP and URL addresses.

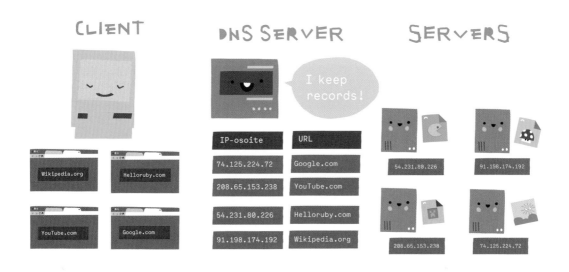

Use the DNS Server list to figure out the IP address of each website Ruby wants to visit. Can you tell which image is shown on each website?

If you run into a page with error message "500 Internet Server Error" it means the server hosting the website is down. A 404 error message means the page can't be found.

Fix the URL

Putting together a URL address is almost like assembling a jigsaw puzzle. Start with the protocol, then add the domain pieces, and complete with a file path, if needed.

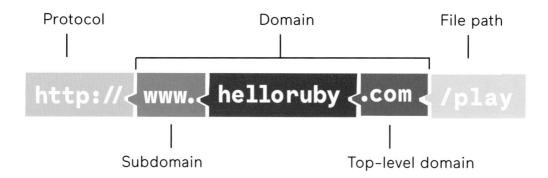

Can you help Ruby create four URL addresses for Hello Ruby with the pieces below? To get everything in the right place, pay attention to the colors and shapes. All URL addresses do not necessarily have pieces in all the different colors.

 Discuss
Visit some of your favorite websites and write down the URL addresses from the address bar. What elements can you find?

INTERNET SERVICES

The Internet is a collection of great technologies. But what really makes the Internet special is the way people can use it to communicate and share things with one another.

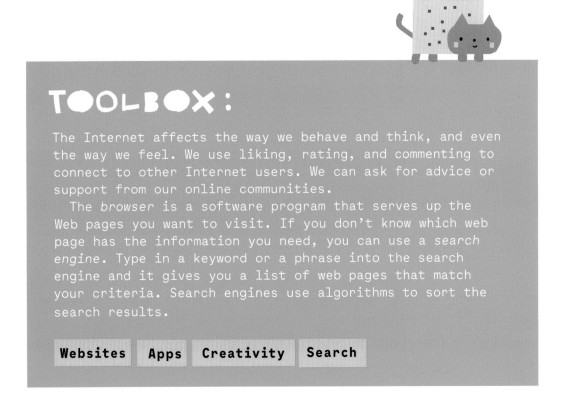

TOOLBOX:

The Internet affects the way we behave and think, and even the way we feel. We use liking, rating, and commenting to connect to other Internet users. We can ask for advice or support from our online communities.

The *browser* is a software program that serves up the Web pages you want to visit. If you don't know which web page has the information you need, you can use a *search engine*. Type in a keyword or a phrase into the search engine and it gives you a list of web pages that match your criteria. Search engines use algorithms to sort the search results.

Websites **Apps** **Creativity** **Search**

Design a Website

You're a web designer. And here are your customers. Can you help them design these sites? Gather inspiration by looking at other websites on the Internet. Draw a wireframe first and then add more details.

I'd like a new website for my ice-cream shop. The page should have a gallery of all the ice-cream flavors. I'd also like the price list and opening times of the shop on the page. Oh, and a map of the location of the store would be great! I'd also like you to use my favorite colors: orange, yellow, and green.

I've just started an animal clinic and I need you to design a website for the customers to reserve times for checkups. Could you also include photos of the pets?

I'd like to start a discussion forum for all my Snow Castle architect friends. We'd like to post photos and be able to comment and rate the different castles.

What's something that you know a lot about? Something that you could teach somebody? Design a website or an app for it.

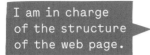I am in charge of the structure of the web page.

HTML

I take care of the looks. CSS

And I can make a web page interactive! JAVASCRIPT

Search engine

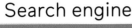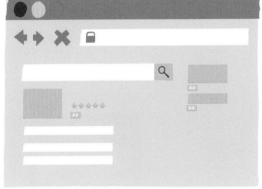

Company website

Online store

Wireframes are how designers try to lay out ideas before putting a lot of time into building the website in detail. They are often drawn on regular paper, with boxes, arrows, and circles.

 You can print a game with HTML, CSS, and Javascript at **helloruby.com/play**

Exercise 19: Apps

Let's Be in Touch

The Internet allows many different ways to communicate, like messages, e-mail, photos, videos, blogs, and product reviews. Different types of communication serve different purposes and require different styles. Take a look at the messages on the following page. First choose the correct media for each message. Then draft a message on a piece of paper. Read the instructions carefully and don't forget the pictures.

Video message
MESSAGE NUMBER:

Instant message
MESSAGE NUMBER:

Photo-sharing app
MESSAGE NUMBER:

E-mail
MESSAGE NUMBER:

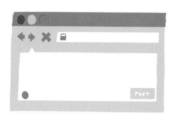

Group discussion
MESSAGE NUMBER:

Web store
MESSAGE NUMBER:

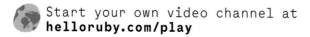

Start your own video channel at
helloruby.com/play

MESSAGE 1

From: Ruby
To: Grandma
What the message is about: Ruby wants to tell about her weekend trip. She has some nice photos she would like to show.
Tips: Grandma likes polite language and doesn't know Internet speak, but she might like an emoji.

MESSAGE 2

From: Ruby
To: Julia
What the message is about: Ruby is going to Django and Julia's house for a slumber party. Ruby's dad wants to know what Ruby should bring with her.
Tips: Dad is in a hurry and wants to know right away what to pack.

MESSAGE 3

From: Ruby
To: Dad
What the message is about: Ruby has learned some new words in Japanese. It is a surprise for Dad, but he is abroad on a business trip.
Tips: Dad might be asleep, or in a business meeting, or might not have Internet. Plan for this!

MESSAGE 4

From: Ruby's soccer coach
To: Parents
What the message is about: Time of soccer practice has been changed.
Tips: The parents have a discussion group.

MESSAGE 5

From: Ruby
To: All Ruby's friends
What the message is about: Ruby took an amazing photo of Django scoring a goal in the game. Now she wants to share it.
Tips: Write a caption for the photo and choose a few funny hashtags. Did you ask for permission from Django to post the photo?

MESSAGE 6

From: Julia
To: Everyone interested in robots
What the message is about: Julia loves her robot and wants to write, together with Mom, a review for the Web shop. She is a little disappointed in the battery life of the robot.
Tips: The review is public, so remember to use proper language. Add stars to Julia's review. Come up with three items people who like Julia's robot might also like.

Art Challenge

Nearly all phones have a camera, and taking photos and videos and sharing them on the Internet is very popular. Now Ruby has a challenge for you. Can you find the following items and either take a picture or draw them in the correct colors?

Something orange that you can eat.

Something powder pink that is in a book or a magazine.

Something green that grows outside.

Something light purple in your school.

A selfie with something yellow in it.

A portrait of your favorite toy against a light green background.

Something purple that you like.

Something light blue that doesn't belong to you.

Something pink that is alive.

Trim the photos or drawings into squares and glue them onto a piece of paper. You can also add captions for them.

Always ask for permission if you post photos of other people on the Internet.

You can share your art with the world at **helloruby.com/play**

Emoji Time

Emoji are images of things like faces, weather, food, animals, and activities we use in text messages, e-mails, and online. Emoji are a way to share our feelings, like humor or affection, in our messages. Because there are only a limited number of emoji in the keyboard, we've started to use them creatively. Emoji have turned into a language of their own.

- **Tell a story.** Sometimes it's hard to tell what each emoji is communicating. Tell a story of a situation where you'd use each of the emoji below.

- **Name it.** Give a name to the feeling behind each of these emoji. Then compare with a friend. Did you come up with different answers?

- **Practice.** Can you make a silly face? What about a confused one? Can your friend guess which emoji you're trying to do?

- **Design.** Make your own emoji. Think about a feeling you've had and how to make it into an emoji. Use materials like paper, cardboard, and glitter.

 You can download an emoji sheet and make masks at **helloruby.com/play**

Scavenger Hunt

Practice problem solving with Ruby and complete the hunt together with an adult. Keep a list of your findings.

- Say "Hello Ruby" in 10 different languages.
- Find a route from your home to your friend's home.
- Learn a new skill by watching a YouTube video.
- Find a recipe for a good chocolate cake and test it!
- Use a weather app to look up the weather forecast for this week.
- Find one historical event that happened on the day you were born.
- How can you find a photo of penguins with red scarfs?
- Find out how many days old you are today.
- Read a news article. Can you find another article with a different view?
- Make the same search for "world's deadliest animal" with two different search engines. Mark down the top results for both search engines. Which ones are the same?

 Find Ruby's tips for searching like a pro at **helloruby.com/play**

Over the Internet many people can work together on a problem and come up with great solutions and ideas. This is called crowdsourcing.

 Discuss

Can you name any web browsers and search engines?

Crawler Alert!

Search engines use tiny software robots known as *web crawlers* or *spiders* to collect information on different pages. A crawler moves from link to link and brings back data to the server. In what order should the crawler go through the websites to collect data on all of them? (Try to land on each site only once!)

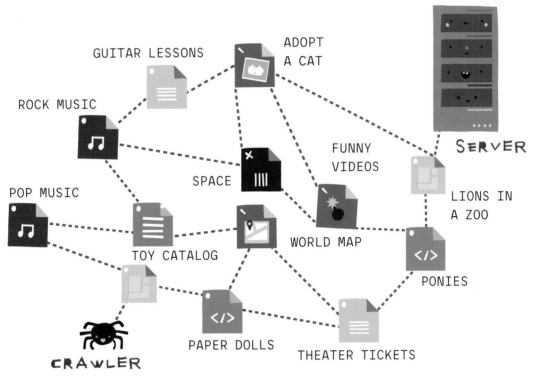

The server uses over 200 pieces of data including keywords, titles, and links to choose the right result. Which of the web pages above would you return for each search query below?

- "Japan location"
- "Lion King London"
- "Satellites"
- "Dolls"
- "Music"
- "Cat videos"

5

WATCH OUT!

There are fun things you can do on the Internet. But not everything you see or hear on the Internet is nice or even true.

TOOLBOX:

Many web services collect data about us. Sometimes it's data we provide ourselves such as our name or e-mail address, and sometimes it's the things we click on.

There are criminal elements active online, and new threats appear every day. That's why security and privacy require alertness. Security is one of the biggest challenges facing the Internet. On the Internet, you can increase security with hardware and software, but in the end it is our own behavior that counts.

| Privacy | Malware | Security |

Ruby's Rules for Safe Surfing:

Not everything online is the truth. Be aware of ads and don't let the trolls make you sad. Always tell a responsible adult if you come across anything that makes you feel uncomfortable.

Personal data is personal. Keep it to yourself. Do not share information such as your address or phone number. Many apps and websites collect information about you. Check out the settings to opt out and choose what access each application gets. Act your age: the services for kids have stricter rules.

The Internet remembers everything. Never write or upload things you don't want to remember in a few years' time.

Cyberbullying is bad. Don't respond to messages that are rude or make you feel uncomfortable, and always tell an adult.

Passwords are good. Learn to make strong passwords and memorize them.

Malware often hides. Check with your parents before downloading or installing apps.

Discuss

Do you have any other rules that you have agreed on at home or at school?

#Dataselfie

We share a lot about ourselves on the Internet. Websites find out your preferences and habits as you use their services. Fill out the following pieces of data about yourself. It's okay, if you haven't done all the things on the list—just skip the unnecessary ones.

5 things you've searched online

4 things you've liked or given a thumbs-up

3 videos you've watched

2 places you've been with a phone

1 person you've messaged

Ask your family members or friends to do the same. Mix the selfies and try to guess who is who based on the data. How old might the person be? Draw a selfie based on the data. Put up the portraits and have a mini art show.

Discuss

Which one of these is a thing you'd share with your best friend? Which one with a stranger?

Download the #dataselfie worksheet at **helloruby.com/play** and practice more

Real or Fake?

Because anyone can say anything on the Internet, you can sometimes run into things that are not true. To be able to tell what is true and what is a lie, pay attention to the source of the information, who wrote it, when it was posted, and what kind of pictures were used.

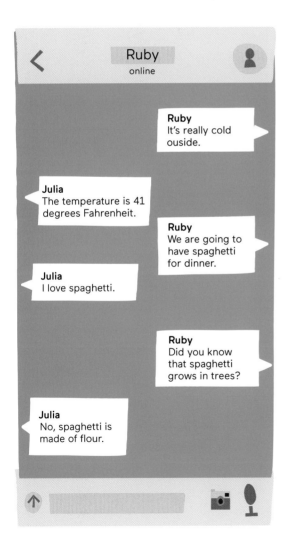

Ruby
online

Ruby
It's really cold ouside.

Julia
The temperature is 41 degrees Fahrenheit.

Ruby
We are going to have spaghetti for dinner.

Julia
I love spaghetti.

Ruby
Did you know that spaghetti grows in trees?

Julia
No, spaghetti is made of flour.

Fact or opinion?
Ruby and Julia are chatting. Which messages are facts and which ones are opinions? Why is a certain statement a fact and another one an opinion?

 **Discuss**

Tell two stories, one of which is true and one that is false. Let your friends ask questions and guess which one of the stories is true. See if you can fool your friends!

Ad or Article?

Web advertisements or ads are announcements about things like toys, food, or games designed to make people want to buy them. The Internet is full of advertisements. Ads make the free Internet possible. But it is not always easy to tell what is an online advertisement.

Here is the web page of Ruby's hometown newspaper. Some of the things that appear on the page are news stories and others are advertisements.

This **is / is not** an advertisement because:

This **is / is not** an advertisement because:

This **is / is not** an advertisement because:

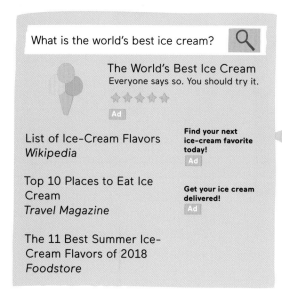

Which of the search results are ads? Which ones are articles? Which one of the search results fits Ruby's search best? Why?

Your browsing history can be tracked and used for marketing purposes. Can you guess which pages Ruby has visited based on the ads that are shown to her?

Free or not?

Free games aren't always free. Sometimes you are asked to do something so you can continue to play. What three things can you spot that make this game not altogether free?

Malware Mayhem

Every day new pieces of malicious software get unleashed online. There are many nasty surprises: there's spyware, trojans, viruses, phishing, and other exploits.

Who did it?

All the characters on the screen have fallen to the bottom of the screen. Use the clues to solve which piece of malware made the mess.

Suspects:

CASCADE   BRAIN   MYDOOM

Eyewitness #1	Eyewitness #2	Eyewitness #3
I'm sure the virus had purple and pink in it.	I think that the virus had either square-shaped eyes or triangle-shaped eyes.	I'm not sure about anything else, but I know the virus didn't have blue in it.

Oh no! The computer has been infected again. This time it's sending TV show quotes as pop-ups on every search result.

Suspects:

STUXNET   SASSER   MELISSA

Eyewitness #1	Eyewitness #2	Eyewitness #3
All I know is that the virus was not purple.	I think the virus had green or blue eyes.	I would say that the virus had a short tail and legs.

DDoS

If a hacker takes over a computer and starts to send too many requests, it slows down the server. This is called a DDoS (Distributed Denial of Service) attack.

Oh no. Two of the computers are sending too many requests for the poor server and the website is down. Can you find which machines are sending more than one request to the server?

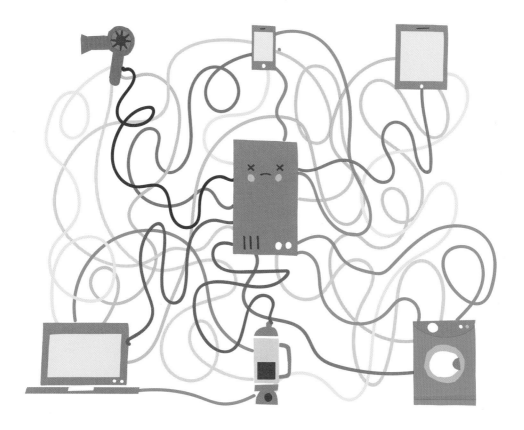

 Discuss

Draw a picture of a virus and name it. How can you protect your computer from catching that particular virus?

Exercise 28: Malware

Phishing

Phishing is an attempt to trick people into thinking a service is real. The fake e-mails and URL addresses can look exactly like the originals. Which of these addresses belong to Hello Ruby? Which ones belong to someone else? You can look at Exercise 17 for help.

https://www.helloruby.com

www.teacher.com/helloruby

www.helloruby.teachers.com

https://www.hellonryby.com

www.helloruby.com/teachers

The letter s stands for "secure" in *https*!

Black hat hackers try to cause trouble. White hat hackers help to find the loopholes in systems.

Keep a Secret!

Most of the information on the Internet is open, which means routers can look at the data in the packets as they pass it on. If you want to send a message on the Internet and keep it secret, it is important to *encrypt* the data first. Encryption is like a code that protects the data as it travels. The data is put back together or *decrypted* when it reaches its destination.

Julia has written two messages and encrypted them using the code key below. In this encryption every picture represents a letter. Can you use the key to decrypt Julia's message?

Message 1

Message 2

You can make your own encryption key at **helloruby.com/play**

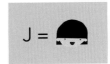

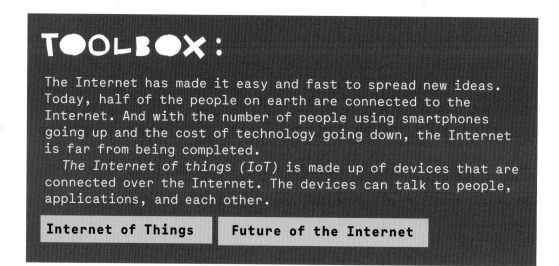

6

IMPACT OF THE INTERNET

The Internet is a miraculous invention. It has quickly changed a lot of things in our lives.

TOOLBOX:

The Internet has made it easy and fast to spread new ideas. Today, half of the people on earth are connected to the Internet. And with the number of people using smartphones going up and the cost of technology going down, the Internet is far from being completed.

The Internet of things (IoT) is made up of devices that are connected over the Internet. The devices can talk to people, applications, and each other.

| Internet of Things | Future of the Internet |

Copy of a Copy of a Copy

The Internet is a copy machine. Every click, every picture, and every action is copied many times when sent over the Internet. Every message is broken down into many copies as it travels through the routers to the servers. And the messages are backed up on many servers. How many copies of each items can you spot?

It's hard to delete anything from the Internet once it's uploaded!

Living Online

Many of the things we do every day have moved onto the Internet. Can you name apps or services that have replaced the following? Is there something that you would like to add to the list?

 BEFORE INTERNET

TASK

 WORLD OF INTERNET

Watching cartoons

Sharing photos

Keeping a journal

Collecting ideas

Calling friends and family

Finding phone numbers and addresses

Listening to music

Talking with friends

Checking the weather

Shopping

Playing games

Paying for things

The Internet is made up of many small pieces loosely connected, so anyone can join and build it. Though, nowadays, many of the online services are owned by big companies.

Everything Is Online

In the future, many of the everyday things we have around us will be connected to the Internet. Match the items in the yellow boxes to the activities in the blue boxes. Imagine what the combination could do online.

bicycle

toothbrush

shoes

umbrella

something else

send message

share location

take a photo

search Internet

sense movement

bicycle

share location

This is what my computer would do if it could access the Internet:

These are examples Ruby came up with:

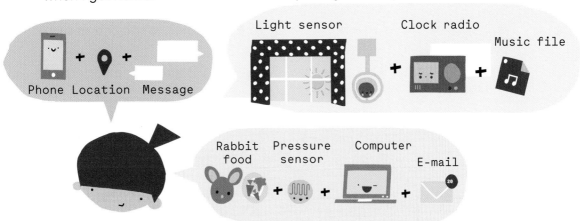

- Notify my family when I get home.

- When the sun rises, open my curtains and play a wake-up song from my clock radio.

Phone   Location   Message

Light sensor   Clock radio   Music file

Rabbit food   Pressure sensor   Computer   E-mail

- Send me an e-mail when my rabbit is hungry.

Build Your Own Internet

All the snow melted during the night and the Snow Internet that Ruby, Julia, and Django created is gone. Now it's your turn to build an Internet. Take a piece of paper and draw a grid similar to the one you see on the following page. Use a ruler to help keep the lines straight.

Julia

Julia's advice for building the Internet
Add the following devices:

- a phone (A4)
- a tablet (B2)
- a laptop (B5)
- a server (D3)
- an unusual item that could be connected to the Internet (A3)
- a router (D4)
- Link all devices together into a computer network. What is this network pattern called? (Hint: Review Exercise 3.)

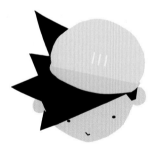

Django

Django's building instructions
Add the following things:

- Computers use a certain networking protocol when talking to each other. Write the name of that protocol (B3).
- Add a DNS Server to C3 and link it together with the device on D3.
- Write the URL address of your favorite web page (C4).
- Add the name of the browser you use (A1).

 You can print the blueprint at
helloruby.com/play

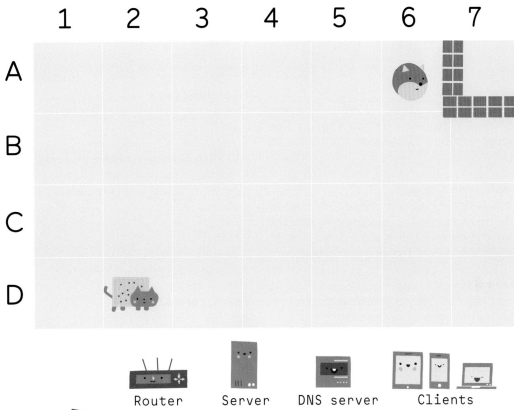

	1	2	3	4	5	6	7
A							
B							
C							
D							

Router   Server   DNS server   Clients

Ruby

Ruby too has a few tips for building the Internet
Add the following:

- To protect your Internet from malware draw a firewall (D7). Add some angry viruses behind the firewall.
- You can see my favorite thing on the Internet on D2. What color is it? Draw a picture of something you like on the Internet (B7).
- Which of the following words best describes your Internet: "gentle," "funny," "serious," "reliable," "scary," "independent," "smart," "exciting." You can also come up with a word of your own. Write the word you choose (B1).
- On the empty spaces you can write or draw new fun things that you have learned about the Internet.

Glossary

Algorithm
An algorithm is a set of specific steps to solve a problem. Search engines like Google or Bing use search algorithms to sort the results.

Application or app
An application is a computer program. Apps can be found on the web, mobile phones, and computers. There are many kinds of apps, from games to word processing.

Bandwidth
The rate at which information travels through an Internet connection.

Browser
A software program that serves up the web pages you want to visit.

Client
A device or software program that uses a service made available by a server. Laptops, tablets, and smartphones are typical examples of clients.

Cloud computing
The delivery of computing services over the Internet. Instead of storing data on our own computers, we use servers to store and calculate data.

Crawler or Spider
A tiny software robot that search engines use to collect information of different web pages.

DNS (Domain Name Service)
The service that translates URLs to IP addresses and the other way around.

Fiber optic cable
Cable that carries data transmitted as light.

HTTP (Hypertext Transfer Protocol)
A protocol for transferring files on the web. HTTPS is the secure version of the protocol.

Internet
A global network of computers where computers can share information.

Internet of things
Devices that are connected over the Internet and can send and receive data from one another.

Internet software
The instructions, protocols, and programs the Internet uses.

IP address
A unique number assigned to any item that is connected to the Internet.

ISP (Internet Service Provider)
A company or an organization that provides Internet access and other Internet services.

Malware
Malware, short for malicious software, is any software used to disrupt the computer. It includes, for example, viruses, phishing attempts, Trojan horses, and other exploits.

Network
A group of interconnected people or things.

Networking hardware
Electrical or mechanical parts of the Internet such as cables, routers, and servers.

Networking protocols
A set of rules for how things work; for example, how data packets move across the Internet. Protocols make sure that all computers on the Internet can understand each other.

Network topology
Different patterns for organizing computer networks. Common network topologies include Star, Bus, Mesh, Ring, Tree, and Physical topology and describe the placement of the various components, and logical topology illustrates how data flows within a network.

Packets
Small chunks of data sent over a network. Messages have to be broken down into data packets before they can travel on the Internet.

Protocol
A set of rules for how things work—for example, how data packets move across the Internet. Protocols make sure that all computers on the Internet can understand each other.

Router
Devices that help information get to the right destinations around the Internet.

Search engine
A program that can help to search information on web pages. Search engines use algorithms to sort the search results.

Server
Computers that store data and provide things to other computers.

TCP/IP (Transmission Control Protocol/Internet Protocol)
One of the main Internet protocols with a step-by-step guide that each computer follows when sending and receiving the data packets.

URL (Universal Resource Locator)
An easy-to-remember address for people to find a web page.

Web (World Wide Web)
The web is not the same as the Internet. The web is a way to access information on the Internet by using a web browser. It consists of a large number of web servers that hosts websites that are linked to one another.

Wi-Fi
A wireless method of sending information using radio waves.

Linda Liukas is a

programmer, storyteller, and illustrator from Helsinki, Finland. She is the author of *Hello Ruby: Adventures in Coding*; *Hello Ruby: Journey Inside the Computer*; and *Hello Ruby: Expedition to the Internet*, which have been sold in over twenty countries. In 2017 Hello Ruby's playful teaching philosophy won DIA Gold, the biggest design award in China.

The idea for Hello Ruby made its debut on Kickstarter and quickly smashed its $10,000 funding goal in just over three hours, becoming one of Kickstarter's most-funded children's books in the process.

Linda is a central figure on the scene of computational thinking. Her TED talk on the topic "A Delightful Way to Teach Children About Computers" has been watched over 1.6 million times. Linda is also the founder of Rails Girls, a global phenomenon teaching the basics of programming to young women everywhere. The workshops, organized by volunteers, have taken place in 270 cities in the past few years.

Linda previously worked at Codecademy, a programming education company in New York City that boasts millions of users worldwide, but left to focus on her children's books, which she believes is one of the best platforms to introduce kids to technology, computers, and computational thinking. Linda has studied business, design, and engineering at Aalto University and product development at Stanford University.

Linda believes that code is twenty-first-century literacy and the language of creativity. Our world is increasingly run by software, and every child has the right to know more about programming. Stories are one way of introducing the world of technology to kids. ◆

lindaliukas.com
@lindaliukas
helloruby.com